The first in the Little 5 Watering Hole series.

"Are We There ...Yet?"

Tiko's first trip to the Kalahari

Kalahari®

ISBN- 978-0-9827982-2-5
Written and Illustrated by Christie Morris of Weber Group, Inc.

Published by Kalahari Resorts

Printed in the USA by Book Masters Inc.
30 Amberwood Parkway, Ashland, Ohio 44805,
July 2012 Job number 9705

"Are we there yet?" Tiko asked for what must have been the 100th time. The baby elephant and his family were traveling across the Great Kalahari Desert in Africa. The sand felt very hot on Tiko's little toes.

The elephants followed an ancient migration route walking from winter feeding grounds to the cool waters of Kalahari's Okavango Delta for summer. They made this trip every year to eat the lush grasses and swim in the refreshing water. Tiko's mom, dad, big sister Patik and big brother Batu had all been there before, but this was the baby elephant's first time.

"I *can't* wait to get there!" Patik said with anticipation. "We're going to have so much fun playing in all that water. Tiko, you're going to feel so big when you make your first big splash!"

Tiko tried to imagine the Great Kalahari Desert having enough water to swim in but all he saw was a sea of sand. The baby elephant curled his trunk to keep it from touching the hot sands, and wished they were already there. He had heard about swimming but had never seen enough water to stomp around in, let alone swim in. The thought of so much water to play in made him smile.

"Imagine a watering hole so big our whole family can swim in it!" exclaimed Patik.

"All of us? Mom? Dad? Big brother Batu? At the same time?" Tiko asked amazed.

"*Even* big brother Batu!" she said.

"Wow!" Tiko said with surprise. "Then there must be a lot of water."

Patik smiled with pride. She was teaching her baby brother about family tradition. She held her head high and continued, "And then we will do the *Pula-Pula*!"

"What's that?" asked Tiko. "A dance?"

"Not *Hula-Hula*." Patik said, "*Pula* means rain!"

"Oh," Tiko puzzled, "so it's a rain dance?"

"No," she said, "*Pula-Pula* is a Celebration of the Great Kalahari Waters! It's when we throw our trunks up in the air and spray water all around like rain."

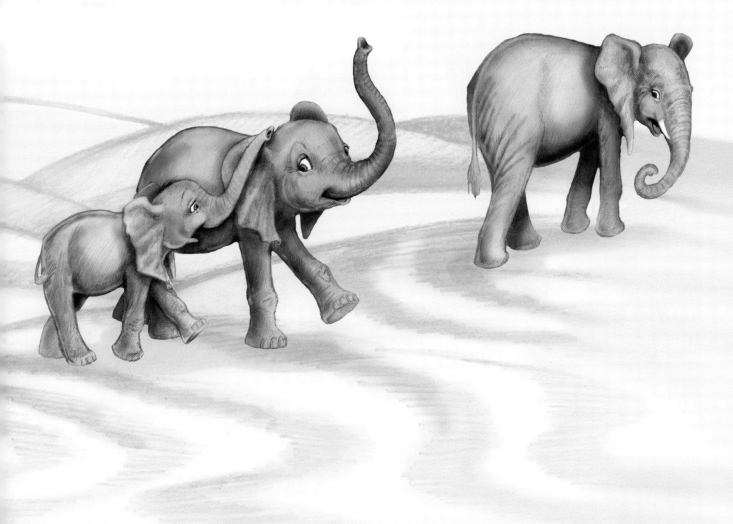

"Do you think I could *Pula-Pula too-la*?" Tiko asked jokingly.

"If you're big enough to swim you're big enough to do the *Pula-Pula*!" Patik promised.

"We've been talking about it so much, I can almost smell the water from here," she said.

Batu calmly said, "Patik, that's because we are close enough that you *can* smell the water."
He was just as excited but trying to act cool since he was the big brother.

Tiko stopped when he heard that, his tail whirling, and asked his favorite question,
"So, are we there yet?"

Big Batu and Patik sighed, saying at the same time, "Almost."

They *were* nearly there, and the elephants began walking faster. Well faster for elephants. They were so excited!

The elephants rounded the last bend in their trail and stopped. There in front of them was a magnificent view of Kalahari's Okavango Delta. Spring rains up in the mountains of Angola sent water down the Okavango River to the thirsty Kalahari Desert. The water transformed the dry sand into a delta, a lush, green oasis, that stretched as far as they could see.

Tiko got thirsty looking at it. He peeked between the tall legs of his mom and dad, smacked his lips and asked, "Are we there yet?"

"Almost, Tiko, almost." Patik said, "But now you can see where we are going. Isn't it wonderful?"

Batu couldn't wait any longer after walking in the heat for many, many miles. There was no holding him back as he charged toward the water! The rest of the elephants chased after Batu towards the leafy trees and shimmering pool.

All at once they splashed into the delta. All except Tiko.

He raced as fast as his little feet could carry him. The closer he got to the pool the bigger the water looked. He stopped at the edge. "Am I really big enough to swim?" he asked his reflection in the water.

Patik, splashing about, called to him, "Come on in Tiko! You can do it! Jump in!"

"Tiko! Tiko! Tiko!" the whole family cheered.

His mom, dad and whole family were swimming together and he wanted to be with them. His feet touched the water. It felt so cool on his hot toes, he no longer worried and jumped in!

The splash *was* big, just like Patik said. Water went everywhere!

"Yay!" Patik squealed! "You just made your first splash into the Okavango Delta!"

Tiko popped his face out of the water. "I didn't know swimming was so much fun!" he said, giggling. "Did you see me?! Did you see my first big splash?!"

Just then, a pudgy little hippo surfaced. "Great splash!" he said. "Hi, my name is Harlo the Hippo."

Patik smiled and said, "This is Tiko, my baby brother. It's his first time here."

"Hey," Tiko argued, "I *am* her brother, but I am *not* a baby!"

Patik rolled her eyes and laughed, "I remember you Harlo. Elephants are very good at remembering. You were here last year."

She continued, "My name is Patik and we are staying to play in the waters of the Kalahari."

"We are here to play too!" Harlo exclaimed. "Have you met Crash yet?"

Tiko and Patik looked at each other then shook their heads.

"Crash is the little rhino over there on shore catching some rays. It's his first trip to the Okavango Delta too!" Harlo said. "He just had lunch and is resting with his mom before coming back in."

"Hey, I just remembered, Crash is part of the Big Five, just like you!" Harlo exclaimed.

Tiko wondered, "The Big Five what?"

"You *are* an elephant, right?" Harlo asked.

"Of COURSE I am an elephant," Tiko said in a grown-up voice.

"Well, the elephant, rhino, lion, leopard and Cape Buffalo are the Big Five African animals." Harlo sat next to Tiko and explained, "And not only are YOU the biggest animal in the Big Five, you are the biggest animal with four legs in the world!"

Just then a voice called from the shore, "Hey Harlo, who's the new little elephant?"

The voice belonged to a lanky little giraffe, standing close to her dad.

"This is Tiko," Harlo said, "and it's his first time in the waters of the Kalahari."

"Nice to meet you! My name is Treesa," the giraffe said batting her long lashes. "Did you have to travel far to get here?"

"Oh yes," sighed Tiko, "we walked over a hundred miles across hot sand but it was worth it to get to swim!"

"Treesa, why don't you come swim with us?" Tiko asked.

"The water isn't deep enough for me to swim where you do because my legs are so long. I can wade all the way across," she explained.

"I'm short enough to swim here!" Harlo demonstrated and blew bubbles from underwater.

"I know what you mean, Treesa," said Patik. "I'm too tall to swim in the shallow water now that I'm bigger. But it's fun for the smaller ones. I swim in the deeper part of the pool."

A Gray Crowned Crane, who was nearby, joined in the conversation. "I like to wade in water shallow enough for me to see my own toes," he said wisely.

Tiko was amazed that the watering hole had areas for everyone to play in, no matter how short or tall.

A little roar came from the opposite shoreline that made Tiko and Patik turn. They saw a lion cub and leopard cub at the water's edge. The tiny cats were splashing each other and clearly having a ton of fun.

Harlo the Hippo popped up from the water and exclaimed, "All the Big Five are here now!"

Tiko shook his head. "No, there are only four; I see the lion, leopard, rhino and elephant—which is me. But where is the Cape Buffalo?"

"Over here," said a voice from the deep water.

Tiko turned to find a huge Cape Buffalo in water that came up to her nose.

"Oh! Hello! I didn't see you there," Tiko said, surprised.

"How could you? So much of me is hidden underwater," the mama buffalo sighed. "I love soaking in the Okavango Delta and so does my little calf, Calli."

"Where is Calli?" asked Tiko. "Is she underwater? I don't see her?"

"Now you see me!" Calli yelled, as she plunged into the water. "Now you don't!" she squealed, peeking out of the water's surface. "You were looking for me, weren't you? I'm Calli the Cape Buffalo!" she said. "I love making a splashy entrance!"

"Did you have to come a great distance to get here?" asked Tiko. "We did. It made my feet hot."

"Oh yes. We walked a long way," said Calli, "but I'm glad to be here now!"

Just then, Batu dragged his trunk through the water and sent sprays flying in all directions. Birds in the distance took to flight, frogs began croaking and the little cats kept splashing. Tiko took it all in and said, "I've never seen a happier place in all my life. This is *so* much fun!"

Patik looked around, "Now, all of the Big Five are here!"

"Wait a minute! You can't have the Big Five without me!" called Crash. The rhino charged into the water, splashing Tiko.

"Don't worry! We already counted you!" Tiko laughed as the water sparkled on his face. "I have never met a rhino before. Hi! My name is Tiko. We got here today!"

Crash swam around the little elephant and said, "We got here yesterday and are staying a long time."

"Good! I'll have plenty of new friends to play with," Tiko said. "Now that I know I'm part of the Big Five I don't ever want to leave."

"We may be part of the Big Five but we are all just little ones compared to our moms and dads," said Patik.

"So are we like the Big Five-Kid's Club?" Tiko asked.

"Yeah," Crash agreed, "we are the LITTLE FIVE!"

Just then, Batu trumpeted the start of the *Pula-Pula* Celebration. Raising his trunk high in the air, he sprayed water down like rain.

Tiko, like all elephants, had a good memory and remembered the long journey. He and his family walked very far to the Okavango Delta and it made him very tired and very thirsty. He could see now, it was worth it. He thought about all he'd done. 'I made my first big splash, made new friends, am part of the Big Five, and now, about to do the *Pula-Pula*.'

Just like his big brother, Tiko drew water in through his trunk, lifted it straight in the air and sprayed the water so it fell like rain.

The rest of the elephants joined in sending water up in every direction. It showered down on everything. Tiko's new friends and the other animals played in the *Pula-Pula* showers.

Tiko put his trunk down to draw more water and thought to himself,
                'I am so glad I am finally HERE!'

Check out our Kalahari Newsletter at
www.kalahariresorts.com/newsletter

Kalahari®